# The Adventures of Ralph, the Superhero Flying Squirrel

By Scott Sindelar

Illustrations by Enrica Mandlemon

D1495237

# Dedication

I dedicate this book to all who enjoy flying, especially those who pilot their own wings.

# Table of Contents

# 1. Ralph is born

Tiny Ralph was born just like all baby flying squirrels are born, hairless, helpless, and frightened. Delicate pale whiskers poked out around his nose. He was snuggled down at the bottom of a nest high up near the top of a ponderosa pine tree. None of his senses worked. He was deaf, blind, and could not smell anything. He was totally dependent upon Mama, his mother. He would not be able to hear for several days. He would not be able to see until he was four or five weeks old. Ralph did not know this, of course. He only knew that he was hungry, very hungry. He was always hungry.

As the nights passed, Mama could always sense his hunger and knew that she must find food for herself so she could suckle her newborn son. Ralph could only drink mother's milk until he was older and could eat solid food. Mama was beautiful, with sleek brown fur and a large fluffy tail. She had huge black eyes that could see far into the night. Flying squirrels are nocturnal creatures, awake at night, and sleeping during the daylight hours. The dark of night helped protect them from their enemies. They only searched for food at night.

Leaning down, Mama kissed Ralph on his cheek. His whiskers told him she was there.

Mama whispered in Ralph's ear, "We are safe now, but we must beware of our enemies."

Flying squirrels, especially baby flying squirrels, had many enemies. Ralph did not know this yet, being only a few nights old, and Mama will have to teach him everything about how to survive in the harsh environment.

Mama continued, "There are tree snakes, owls, martens, fishers, coyotes, bobcats, raccoons, and feral cats. They all want to eat us, so we must stay safe in our nest." He was learning to hear, but Ralph did not know what any of these things were. Mama did know, so she carefully scanned their surroundings. Seeing and hearing no danger, she told Ralph, "I must find food. I will be right back."

"Mama! Don't leave me here alone," Ralph cried.

"You are safe here, Ralph, and I'll be back soon," Mama said as she unfurled her wings and sniffed the night air. Her highly developed sense of smell told her that a treasure trove of pine nuts was waiting in a nearby shrub. She feared to leave her baby, but she knew she needed nourishment from food if they were to survive.

Launching into the darkness, Mama soared, circling downward toward the shrub. At the last moment, she flared her wings, using her fluffy tail as an additional air brake. Flying squirrels cannot really fly, or flap their wings like birds to gain altitude. They can only glide from perch to perch.

The furry parachute-like membrane between her front and back limbs was named (by humans) the "patagium," or the plural patagia. These flaps would catch air as she launched off a tree, allowing her to propel herself forward instead of plummeting.

She landed delicately on the top of the shrub. Minutes later, her cheeks were filled with delicious pine nuts. She sniffed the air and searched the darkness for any signs of danger. Sensing none, she launched herself back toward the ponderosa pine.

Mama landed near the base of her tree and scurried upwards to the nest. Ralph was shivering from the cold. Mama covered him with her warm body and nursed her baby until he fell sound asleep.

# Glossary

(A list of words found in a specific text, with explanations; a brief dictionary.)
Ponderosa pine: a large coniferous (evergreen) pine tree. The bark helps to distinguish it from other species. They have yellow to orange-red bark in broad to very broad plates with black crevices.

Nocturnal: done, occurring, or active at night.

Martens: mammals with bushy tails and large paws with partially retractable claws. The fur varies from yellowish to dark brown. Martens are slender, agile animals, and inhabit coniferous and northern deciduous forests across the Northern Hemisphere.

Fishers: a small, carnivorous (meat-eating) mammal native to North America. It is a member of the weasel family.

Feral: an animal in a wild state, especially after escape from captivity or domestication.

Trove:  a collection or store of valuable or delightful things.

## 2. Danger from above

Dawn was still hours away. With a full belly, Ralph was happy and warm at the bottom of the nest. Mama dozed with one eye open, always alert for potential danger. In the crisp, cold night, the stars twinkled above the nest. Then she saw it. A faint shadow crossed the nest. Mama's second eye popped open as she sniffed the air. The fur along her back stood up. Peering into the dark sky, she searched for the source of the ominous shadow.

There it was. Circling high above the ponderosa pine forest flew one of their mortal enemies! It was a rare spotted owl, searching for prey. Without a second thought, Mama launched out of the nest. She knew that she was no match for the owl, but she had to draw it away from her sleeping baby. She must protect her Ralph!

Mama twisted and turned as she soared through the air toward a neighboring ponderosa. The spotted owl spotted her. Tucking its long wings close to his body, the owl maneuvered into a steep dive, speeding toward Mama.

*Good,* Mama thought, *come and find me.* She flared her patagia at the last moment, hitting hard against the rough bark of the tree. Scrambling around to the other side, Mama ducked inside of a shallow hole in the side of the tree. She could barely turn around, but once she did, she hunkered down, remaining motionless. She knew the owl's keen eyes could discern the slightest movement.

The owl landed on a branch only several feet away. It turned its head around and around, its large eyes searching for his prey. Mama held her breath, hoping the owl would give up. The owl stopped moving. He was looking right at her! Mama did not move. She did not blink. *I am one with the tree*, she thought. *I am the tree.*

The owl's head turned slightly, looking down. Pushing off the branch, the owl launched himself downward. His huge claws reached out and snatched a tiny mouse from the forest floor. The mouse had no idea what hit him as the owl beat its wings and flew off towards his nest. Mama took a deep breath and crawled out of her hiding place. Clawing her way upward, she reached the top of the tree to see if the danger had passed. The owl was nowhere to be seen. Mama unfurled her patagia and glided silently back to her nest. Ralph stirred and let out a high-pitched peep. "Shush, little one. You are safe," Mama said.

"I'm hungry, Mama," Ralph said. "Of course you are," Mama replied. She sighed and launched out into the darkness again. Her foraging would never end.

## Glossary

<u>Dozed</u>: slept lightly.

<u>Potential</u>: having or showing the capacity to become or develop into something in the future.

<u>Ominous:</u> giving the impression that something bad or unpleasant is going to happen; threatening.

<u>Maneuvered</u>: move skillfully or carefully.

<u>Keen:</u> (of a sense) highly developed.

<u>Discern</u>:  To percieve or recognize something.

<u>Foraging</u>:  Searching for food.

# 3. Mama Teaches Ralph to Fly

Ralph was now five weeks old, and it was time to learn to fly! He trembled with excitement. Mama had carried him to one of the lower branches of their ponderosa. He clung to the branch, his little claws digging into the bark. It smelled like vanilla, as ponderosas often do. Ralph was now covered with soft brown fur. His head seemed too large for his body, and his eyes covered most of his face. Mama said, "Unfurl your patagia, my son."

Ralph did as he was told, but the fur along his back stood up, signaling the fear he felt inside. Looking toward the ground, he could only think of his impending death, envisioning his body splattered on the forest floor below. Mama smiled and said, "Ralph, just watch closely and follow me." She launched gracefully and flew a long way before flaring her patagia and landing next to a bush. She smiled at Ralph encouragingly.

*It looks easy,* Ralph thought. He crouched down, took a deep breath, and pushed himself off into the air. Ralph screamed as he folded his patagia in fear and plummeted downward. The ground came up fast, and he closed his eyes just before hitting a pile of pine needles. He tumbled and rolled before coming to a stop. His fur was covered in dirt and pine needles. Mama hopped over to him. Seeing that he was unharmed, she said, "Let's try that again. This time, keep your patagia unfurled." Ralph nodded sheepishly - even though he was a flying squirrel and not a sheep. They scrambled up to the launching platform to try again.

Mama shouted, "Hey look, Ralph! I'm a flying squirrel!" She launched and glided with ease until landing next to the bush. This time, Ralph kept his patagia open when he launched.

"Whoa, I'm gliding!" he exclaimed, just before crashing into the bush. Mama shook her head but was smiling. Climbing out of the bush, Ralph had a big grin on his face. "That was thrilling!"

Mama said, "Stay here. Now this time, watch how I land." She scrambled back up to the launching pad and repeated her short flight.

Ralph and Mama spent the next days and weeks practicing flying. Each time they climbed higher before launching. Before long, Ralph could glide from the very top of their ponderosa and circle around and around before touching down softly. He learned to sniff out food all the while keeping watch for their dangerous enemies. Soon he was almost fully grown.

## Glossary

Impending: (of an event regarded as threatening or significant) about to happen; forthcoming.

Unfurl: make or become spread out from a rolled or folded state, especially to be open to the wind.

# 4. Ralph Learns to Store Food for the Winter and Hard Times

As summer was nearing its end, Mama and Ralph spent their nights together, foraging for food. Ralph had left the nest many months ago. He learned that he was omnivorous, meaning that flying squirrels could eat almost everything. He could eat seeds, insects, grubs, spiders, shrubs, flowers, fungi, and even tree sap.

His favorite food, however, was pine nuts, the tiny nuts that grew on piñon trees. Several species of pine produced seeds large enough to be worth harvesting, and Ralph became a champion pine nut finder. Hidden inside pinecones are pine nuts, with two nuts under each pinecone scale. The nuts are covered by a hard shell that Ralph could break with his sharp teeth. It was a lot of work to finally get to one of the tiny nuts, but Ralph thought it was worth it to obtain the creamy morsels inside.

Mama taught Ralph the wisdom of eating two but always saving one. He saved hundreds of pine nuts still in their shells for protection from the elements and other living creatures of the forest. He spent many hours finding hiding places for their stash of food.

He had to be clever, as ground squirrels often found his hiding places and stole his hard-earned hoard. Ground and tree squirrels were known to be lazy, spending their days running, jumping, and playing amongst themselves. They were diurnal mammals, awake during daylight hours. When winter came, many of them died of starvation. Mama told him that flying squirrels were industrious and smarter than most other creatures. They were survivors.

*Eat two - save one* became like a mantra for him.

Ralph now had huge, beautiful, round eyes. His disproportionately plump peepers could gather enough light to be able to see in almost total darkness.

Mama taught him another trick. The cartilage spurs at each wrist could be extended almost like an extra finger, stretching out the patagia farther than their tiny arms could on their own.

He could glide over 200 feet. Ralph pushed himself harder each day, practicing aerial aerobatics mostly for fun, but his skills came in handy for eluding flying predators.

Sitting on a branch near the top of a tall ponderosa, he often watched the owls, and sometimes red-tailed hawks and black ravens flying at dawn. Many times, he had tried flapping his patagia mimicking how the birds flapped their wings, but still, he could not truly fly. He was envious of the apparent freedom the birds possessed.

*Still*, he thought, *it is a better life up here than the one down there with the ground squirrels.*

## Glossary

<u>Foraging</u>: searching widely for food or provisions.
<u>Fungi</u>: any of a group of spore-producing organisms (living things)

feeding on organic (plant and animal) matter, including molds, yeast, mushrooms, and toadstools.

Species: a class of things of the same kind.

Stash: to store, in a usually secret place, for future use.

Hoard: a stock or store of money or valued objects, typically one that is secret or carefully guarded.

Diurnal: active during the daytime rather than at night.

Mantra: a word or sound repeated to aid concentration in prayer or meditation.

Disproportionately: to the extent that is too large or too small in comparison with something else.

Plummeting: fall or drop straight down at high speed.

Cartilage: a tough, flexible connective tissue, that reduces friction between joints, holds bones together, and helps support weight.

Aerial: existing, happening, or operating in the air.

Aerobatics: the practice of flying maneuvers involving aircraft attitudes (orientation or position relative to the horizon) that are not used in normal flight.

Eluding: to evade or escape from an enemy.

Predators: an animal that naturally preys on others.

# 5. Ralph gets bored

The sun had disappeared behind the distant mountains long before Ralph awoke. His mother had been foraging for an hour. Mama had tried to awaken him earlier, but he rolled over and went back to sleep.

Ralph felt grumpy and out of sorts. He was tired of foraging night after night. He was tired of eating the same old food, He was tired of finding hiding places for their winter stash. His only enjoyment was doing aerobatics and eating pine nuts.

Climbing out of his own nest, an old nest that he had found abandoned by some large bird, he thought he saw a shadow. He became fully awake and alert. He froze in place. Out of the corner of his eye, he saw a shape flying toward him from one of the tallest trees in the forest.

Stepping up to the edge of the nest, he prepared to launch when he heard Mama's chirping. Landing gracefully on the branch, she looked at him out of the corner of one eye. She said, "Oh, excuse me. I thought you were a tree squirrel, sleeping the night away. You are lucky I wasn't an owl."

Ralph hung his head and mumbled under his breath, "I knew it was you." Mama ignored him, "Why aren't you out gathering food?"

Ralph kicked a stray twig out of the nest, watching it tumble to the ground.

"I'm tired of spending all my nights gathering food. There is never anything else to do around here."

"So, we are bored, are we?" Mama thought a moment. "Well, why not glide over to your grandfather's nest? He could use your help in gathering food." Ralph made an ugly face, which was not easy for a flying squirrel.

"Grandpapa is so old. He has ugly scars all over his body, and he smells funny," Ralph whined. "He talks funny too; he calls me Rodent."

Mama stiffened. "Your Grandpapa earned those scars. He and your father, along with my brothers, your uncles, fought a terrible battle against a pair of owls that once tried to eat me. It was the most frightening night of my life." Mama stared into the distance and shuddered. "That was the night your father died." Looking back at Ralph, she added, "And that smell is the smell of wisdom. Your Grandpapa knows many things I cannot teach you."

Ralph perked up. "He knows things? What kinds of things?" Mama shrugged, "You will have to ask him yourself. Maybe if you help him, you will learn a thing or two." Ralph sniffed the air and scanned the sky above, just as Mama taught him to do. "Okay, okay, Maaaaammuh. I'll go help him now." With that, he launched himself into the darkness.

# 6. The Edge of the Forest

Grandpapa lived at the edge of the forest, on a small peninsula overlooking a turquoise-colored lake. Ralph had to climb many trees and glide extended flights to eventually land near the base of the scraggly conifer pine that Grandpapa called home. Looking down from his nest, Grandpapa called down to him. "I saw you coming from a mile away. Get up here, my careless little rodent," he growled. Ralph clawed his way up the tree and hopped into the nest. Grandpapa squinted at him for a moment and said, "My, my, Ralph. You're all growed up. I guess I can't call you Rodent anymore."

Ralph straightened up, trying to make himself taller. "Hiya, Grandpapa. Mama said you could use my help." He noticed that Grandpapa had a hard time standing and was a little stooped. His nest was shabby, and there were holes in the floor. Grandpapa saw him looking at the nest and said, "Be careful where you walk. You could fall clean through. I've meant to get that fixed, but food is scarce out here, and it takes me all night to get enough to feed me and build my stash."

"I can help you with that, Grandpapa. I saw lots of twigs at the base of your tree." Grandpapa nodded and said, "I will keep watch so you can concentrate on your work." Without hesitating, Ralph launched himself. circling the tree several times before landing on the thick pile of needles and pinecones under the tree. He grabbed a small branch that still had green needles and carried it up to the nest.

Ralph repeated this process for hours, as it took a long time climbing up to reach the shabby nest. Before dawn, the nest looked like new, with soft green pine needles making a nice warm bed for Grandpapa.

Grandpapa smiled broadly as he looked at his renovated home. "You sure are a good grandson,

Ralph. I had plumb forgotten what it is like to have a soft bed. Thank you." He added, "You must be all tuckered out. I set out a pile of pine nuts for you. Your mother said those were your favorite." Ralph realized that he was very hungry, but he was also very tired. "I am happy to help you, Grandpapa. I was getting bored at home and needed a change of scenery." Stretching his arms over his head, he yawned and sat next to the pile of nuts.

Grandpapa said, "Helpin' others is always a good antidote to many negative feelin's. Boredom, depression, anxiety, and even anger can be relieved when we focus on helpin' others." Ralph cocked his head, "I never thought of it that way. I only know I feel a lot better, even though I am very tired." He closed his eyes and soon was sound asleep.

## Glossary

<u>Peninsula</u>: a piece of land jutting out, nearly surrounded by water.

Turquoise: a greenish-blue color.

Conifer: a tree that bears cones and needle-like or scale-like leaves that are typically evergreen.

Rodent: a gnawing mammal of an order that includes rats, mice, squirrels, hamsters, porcupines, and their relatives, distinguished by strong constantly growing incisors and no canine teeth. They constitute the largest order of mammals.

Renovated: restore (something old, especially a building) to a good state of repair.

Antidote: a medicine that is taken or given to counteract (act against or neutralize) a particular poison.

Depression: feeling of severe sadness, unhappiness, sorrow.

Anxiety: a feeling of worry, nervousness, or unease, typically about an imminent (about to happen) event or something with an uncertain outcome.

# 7. Ralph Gets a Shock

Many hours later, Ralph was being shaken awake. The sun had not yet set, and the top of the conifer was still bathed in its yellow rays. Grandpapa was kneeling over him, shaking his shoulder. "What is it, Grandpapa? Are we in danger?"

"No Ralph, we are relatively safe here. I wanted to show you somethin' while the ground is still hot." Ralph stood up, sniffing the air and searching the still blue sky. The bright light hurt his eyes. "I don't understand. What are you talking about?" Ralph was getting worried about his grandfather. *Is he losing his mind?*

"I am gettin' old, Ralph. I may not live through another winter. Your father died before I could pass down some of the ancient secrets of our forefathers. He might have lived longer if he knew some of the secrets, but I was always too busy to teach him. I learned things from my grandfather, and he learned these things from his grandfather before him."

Ralph said, "Mama told me you knew some things you could teach me, but she never said what they were. What kind of secrets are you talking about?"

Grandpapa sniffed the air and looked to the skies. "It'll be better if I show you." Grandpapa stepped to the edge of the nest.

Ralph shouted, "Wait, Grandpapa. We cannot leave the nest while the sun is still up. It's *too dangerous*." He reached out to stop him, but his grandfather spread his patagia and pushed off into the daylight. He soared outward and barely lost altitude. Ralph's eyes grew wide despite the bright light of the sun. *What is happening? Why isn't he gliding downward?*

Grandpapa bounced a little and then started turning in a steep bank. His grandfather should have been dropping out of the sky, but instead, he was going up! He spiraled around and around and kept gliding higher and higher.

Ralph's mouth hung open. He could not believe what he was seeing. Grandpapa continued to spiral upward, his figure becoming smaller until Ralph could barely see him. Finally, Grandpapa reached the flat base of a puffy cloud. He then flew straight out, starting to lose altitude until he was far below the next cloud. Ralph knew Grandpapa would never be able to glide all the way back to the nest, and he prepared to fly down to meet him on the ground.

Instead, Grandpapa banked again and started turning. Once again, he started climbing higher until he reached the base of the cloud. He made a final turn, tucked his patagia and shot down at an insane speed until he was soaring a hundred feet over the nest. He blasted by the tree, and

Ralph thought he was going to crash into the ground.

Grandpapa spread his patagia at the last moment and soared upward one more time, making a steep bank before gliding back to the nest. He landed gracefully and collapsed into his bed. He started laughing and seemed years younger to Ralph.

Grandpapa tried to talk but was laughing too hard. He started coughing, so he leaned back and began to calm himself. Ralph was speechless, and his mouth still hung open. Looking up at Ralph, Grandpapa said, "Close your mouth, son, or you'll catch a bumblebee." Ralph closed his mouth but opened it up again. "What was that? How did you do that?"

Still smiling, Grandpapa finally answered him. "That, Ralph, is what is called thermalling. Our ancestors watched the eagles and certain other birds who do this as a way to gain altitude without flappin' their wings. We can do it as well, but you have to train your senses. Legend has it that way back when, a brave flyin' squirrel was the first ever to catch a thermal and fly like the birds. He could see danger comin' from a long way off. He became a superhero in our forest. Legend also has it that someday he will return,"

He leaned forward, "First, you have to learn to find a thermal. You gotta smell the air and feel the temperature changes. Hot air smells a might different, rises in a spiral, and often ends in a cloud. You can sometimes see dust and small particles risin' and spinnin' around. If you glide into one and start a-turnin', you too can rise with the wind!"

Ralph looked up at the puffy clouds. They seemed so high and far away.  Grandpapa added, "It takes some practice to get the bank angle just right, but when you do, you will feel joy and elation like nothin' else. Then you will know the freedom of the birds."

# 8. Ralph Learns a Secret

"But, Grandpapa, when you were coming back, you tucked your patagia instead of gliding. I've never seen one of us fly so fast."

Grandpapa thought for a moment. "I can't explain it, Ralph. It is a secret technique you have to experience and practice. When you open you patagia at high speeds, you'll have the power to rise higher. My grandfather said it had somethin' to do with the conservation of energy. I never understood it. I only know it works. Are you ready to give her a try? The ground is still mighty hot."

Ralph and his grandfather climbed up to the edge of the nest. Grandpapa glanced at Ralph, "Follow me if you can, little rodent." He launched outward, and Ralph quickly followed on his tail. Ralph could not believe his own eyes. He was not sinking and the air was bumpy. He watched Grandpapa bank and turn and start to fly higher. Ralph mimicked his grandfather's movements.

Soon, they were flying and soaring and even touched the bottoms of clouds. Ralph was surprised to learn the clouds were not solid. They felt like fog, cooler and wetter than the air below.

Now, Ralph could see the ends of the Earth in all directions. The world was so huge. Ralph had never experienced such joy! He had no difficulty sniffing out thermals and quickly learned how to bank for maximum lift.

When Grandpapa said it was time to leave, they tucked their patagia and sped toward the nest at an incredible speed. Ralph had to squint his eyes as the airspeed hurt his delicate eye membranes.

Ralph saw the ground coming up fast and became terrified. He remembered what Grandpapa had told him and snapped open his patagia. This was incredible! He was now soaring up, and almost went into a loop, flying upside down before turning over and gliding to the nest. Grandpapa landed a few seconds later.

"Well?" Grandpapa asked. They looked at each other for a second, and both of them burst out laughing. Ralph said, "Grandpapa, with everything you taught me, I will never be bored again." Grandpapa had a twinkle in his eye -- or maybe it was a tear.


# Glossary

Insane: exhibiting a severely disordered state of mind, crazy.

Thermalling: riding upward movements of hot spiraling air.

Altitude: the vertical elevation of an object above the surface.

Thermals: an upward current of warm air, used by gliders, balloons, and birds to gain height.

Elation: great happiness and exhilaration.

Conservation: prevention of wasteful use of a resource.

Conservation of Energy: This law means that energy can neither be created nor destroyed; rather, it can only be transformed or transferred from one form to another.

Maximum: as great, high, or intense as possible or permitted.

Membranes: a thin sheet of tissue or layer of cells acting as a boundary, lining, or partition; it allows some things to pass through but stops others.

# 9. The Owl Attacks

Ralph spent the night gathering more food. With the two of them working, his Grandpapa would almost have enough food to get through the winter. Already, the nights were getting colder as winter approached. Daylight was emerging. Ralph was tired, but still so excited about learning how to find thermals and soar to the clouds, that he could not sleep. Grandpapa was snoring in the corner of the nest. Ralph decided to stay awake so that Grandpapa could rest.

Ralph saw the world differently now. He was no longer a prisoner of gravity. He began to imagine himself traveling great distances, exploring strange new places, and meeting new creatures all over the world. He had no idea how big the world was, but he planned to find out. His imagination soared, but his eyelids grew heavy, and soon he began to dream.

Ralph was startled awake by the violent rocking of the nest. He heard his Grandpapa screaming. A large spotted owl was inside the nest, and his claws were ripping away at his Grandpapa! The owl was huge, but Ralph jumped on his back and began biting the owl's neck. The owl turned his head around 180 degrees and started snapping at Ralph with his sharp beak. Ralph was agile and quick and managed to avoid being bitten, but he was losing his grip on the owl's slippery feathers.

The owl spun his body around, his powerful wings knocking Ralph out of the nest. He fell upside down, slamming into a lower branch before digging his claws into the bark and stopping his fall. The screams and commotion were heard deep into the forest, and soon two flying squirrels glided toward the conifer to join the fight. They landed near the base of the tree and began climbing upward.

Ralph scrambled up and reached the nest ahead
of them. His grandpapa was on his back; his
chest torn and bleeding. Ralph again jumped
onto the owl's back, attacking him with a
ferocity he didn't know was in him. The other
two squirrels climbed into the nest and began
biting the owl's legs. Feeling outnumbered, the
owl shook them off and launched out of the
nest, with Ralph still on his back!

The owl's strong wings carried them high into
the night sky. The owl twisted and turned,

trying to shake him off. Ralph hung on and continued biting the owl's neck. His feathers were too thick, so Ralph barely caused any damage. The owl tucked his wings and turned upside down. Ralph lost his grip and began falling. The owl flipped over and began beating his wings, flying with a vengeance to attack Ralph in midair.

Seeing the owl flying toward him, Ralph tucked his patagia and began picking up speed. Diving toward the ground with the owl gaining on him, Ralph waited until the last moment before snapping open his patagia, pulling out of the dive, and looping above and behind the owl.

The owl was so focused on catching Ralph that he didn't see the ground coming up fast. Unable to correct his flight in time, he smashed into the ground, breaking his neck. Ralph landed next to him. Seeing he was dead, Ralph scampered to the tree and climbed up to the nest. The two squirrels were looking down at Ralph's grandfather. Seeing Ralph climbing into the nest, they bowed their heads. Grandpapa was dead.

# Glossary

Emerging: move out of or away from something and come into view.

Ferocity: the state or quality of being ferocious.

Focused: pay particular attention to or concentrate on something.

# 10. Ralph the Superhero

The tale of Ralph's bravery and flying skills spread through the forest. Whenever creatures saw Ralph, they bowed their heads.

"Why are they acting like that around me?" Ralph asked. Mama thought a long time before answering. "You have done something amazing, Ralph," she said. "There is an ancient legend about a special flying squirrel. It was said he could truly fly like the birds. Because of his flying skills, he could rise up high above the forest and see danger coming from a long distance away. It is said that he defeated the Owl King. He was a Superhero to them. He died long ago, but it is said that someday he would return when the forest mammals needed his protection." Ralph just shook his head.

Mama said, "Think about it, Ralph. You somehow are able to fly above the trees. You also defeated an owl. Maybe they think you are the reincarnation of that ancient Superhero." Ralph just stared at his feet.

His Grandpapa was dead because of him. He had fallen asleep when he should have been on watch, guarding the nest. He tried to tell them, but the others would just clap him on the back and they started calling him the superhero owl-killer. Meanwhile, the grateful forest mammals knit him a red shirt with a big golden R on the front. Ralph did not feel like a Superhero.

Ralph was still very sad. He and his Mama were grieving, each in their individual ways. Ralph stopped eating and often sat alone in his nest. He had no energy to help Mama with the foraging. Mama dealt with her grief by working harder than ever, gathering enough food for both of them.

After a few nights, Mama knew she needed to do something. She made Ralph tell her about the nights leading up to Grandpapa's death. After he finished, she was silent for a long time. Looking at Ralph she said, "I never learned those things from my parents. I had heard heard about the legend of a flying squirrel who could ride the thermals, but I thought they were just stories for children." She added, "I do not know if your father learned these things, but they did not save him. You must be careful, Ralph. Do not overestimate your skills."

Ralph nodded and started to lie down again. "Wait, just a minute, young squirrel," she said. What did Grandpapa teach you about negative emotions?" Looking down, he mumbled, "I don't know." With her hands on her hips, Mama said, "That is not true. You do know. You had better move forward if you don't want his legacy to be meaningless. Do you think he'd want you to sit around moping all night?"

Ralph had tears running down his furry cheeks, "But it was my fault, Mama. He's dead because of me." Mama replied, "No, Ralph, he would have been killed whether or not you were there. He lived all alone in that nest, and the owl would have killed him anyway. You just happened to be there when it happened. You made him very happy at the end of his life."

Ralph was puzzled. He had not thought of it that way. He felt a weight lifting off his chest. "I guess you are right, Mama." She huffed, "Of course I'm right, Ralph. I'm your Mama. Now, let's get to work."

Soon Ralph was putting all his energy into foraging for himself and Mama, and helping others whenever he could. He taught others to "**eat two and save one**." Some of the parents encouraged him to wear his shirt with a big R in front. They told him that their children looked up to him and tried to emulate him. He was the superhero they had waited for and needed. Even

the most recalcitrant children were starting to
help others and practiced their gliding skills
with renewed energy.

The next day, Ralph wore his shirt for the first
time. The other squirrels cheered when they
saw him. The younger squirrels began following
him around. They asked his advice about how to
find the best nuts and where to stash their food.
Ralph was a natural leader!

# Glossary

<u>Reincarnation</u>: the rebirth of a soul into a new body.

<u>Emotions</u>: feelings, moods.

<u>Legacy:</u> a thing handed down by a predecessor, inheritance, gift.

<u>Emulate</u>: to try to equal or excel; imitate.

<u>Recalcitrant</u>: stubborn, uncooperative attitude toward authority or discipline.

# 11. Invasion of the Beetles

The flying squirrels were almost finished storing their food. At times, Ralph would sneak away and practice finding thermals, soaring up to the clouds.

As the first snowflakes of winter started falling, a contingent of flying squirrels from the south arrived in the forest. They were in great distress. "Our trees are dying. Our seeds, lichen, fruits, nuts, and even our fungi are disappearing." The word spread quickly throughout the forest. A council meeting was called to meet at first darkness.

Mammals from far and wide came to the meeting. A dozen young flying squirrels were tasked with climbing up the tallest trees to keep watch for any predators. This was Ralph's first council meeting, but he was one of the first to be invited. His reputation has spred throughout the forest. Now they came to Ralph for help.

The chosen representative from the southern flying squirrels addressed the council. He was old, with gray fur. He repeated what they said when they first arrived. "Our forest is dying. We have little food for the winter as our resources have disappeared."

An elder from the ground squirrels spoke first. "Do you have any idea what is causing this disaster?" The representative conferred with his contingent. Turning back to the council, he said, "As far as we can tell, it started when a large group of beetles asked to come into our habitat. They were small, and they seemed relatively harmless. They even helped us at times by bringing in fertilizer for our saplings."

Ralph spoke up, resulting in scowls from the elders. "So, what is the problem? You said they were harmless and helpful."

The representative continued, "They were, at first, but within weeks there was a literal invasion of tens of thousands of those beetles. Many were Pine Beetles that normally keep the forests healthy by attacking old or weakened trees. In huge numbers, however, they start attacking healthy trees!"

The mammals murmured among themselves. The old squirrel continued, "They started laying eggs under the bark. Their eggs carry a dangerous fungus that gets into the sapwood. The fungus prevents the tree's pitch flow from repelling and killing the attacking beetles. The fungus also blocks the water and nutrient transport within the tree. The trees start dying within weeks. By the time we figured this out it was too late."

Mama, who was a representative of the flying squirrels, spoke up. "Did you ask them to leave, to go back to their home forest?" The gray furred squirrel replied, "Yes. I spoke to their leader, a nasty, mean, and aggressive beetle called Bruno. We asked them to leave and offered to help them get back to their homes. It was then that they told us that their homeland was barren. Bruno told me that what they had been doing to our forest was the same thing they did to their own forests. They are hungry and have to keep moving into new lands. He only cares about feeding his own." He looked around at the council members. "They will invade our forest next."

# Glossary

Lichen: a simple slow-growing plant that typically forms a low crusty, leaflike, or branching growth on rocks, walls, and trees.

Contingent: a group united by some common feature or purpose.

Council: a group of people who come together to consult, deliberate, or make decisions.

Representative: consisting of a person chosen to act and speak on behalf of a wider group.

Address: a speech or written statement, usually formal, directed to a particular group of persons.

Resources: a source of supply, support, or aid, especially one that can be readily drawn upon when needed.

Conferred: to consult together; compare opinions; carry on a discussion or deliberation.

Habitat: the natural home or environment of an animal, plant, or other organisms.

Fertilizer: a chemical or natural substance added to soil or land to increase its fertility/productiveness.

Saplings: young trees, especially those with slender trunks.

Literal:  factual, matter-of-fact, no-nonsense, unsentimental.

Sapwood: outer, living layers of the wood of trees, which engage in the transport of water and minerals.

Pitch: a sticky resinous black or dark brown substance that is semiliquid when hot, hard when cold.

Nutrient: a substance that provides nourishment essential for growth and the maintenance of life.

Aggressive: ready or likely to attack or confront.

# 12. The Battle of the Beetles

The council met all night until the sky began to lighten in the east. All sides made eloquent arguments. Ralph was impressed with the civility of the debates. Everyone's opinion was respected no matter how deep the differences of opinions. Soon the outcome became obvious to all.

The council Chair-mammal stood and addressed all the mammals in attendance. "Ladies and gentle-mammals, despite all our differences, over the centuries we have learned to live together in relative harmony. Ancient tales spoke of the great awakening when our ancestors decided to stop fighting amongst themselves. We have prospered, and our forest has prospered from our collective caretaking. We have done well by *taking one and planting two.*"

He looked around at each of their faces. "Efforts to appease this growing and evil threat have resulted in disaster. Their leader will not, or cannot listen to reason. We now face a horrible but clear choice. We either welcome the starving beetles into our forest and face the imminent destruction of our trees and food sources, and ultimately our lives, or we fight the invaders and drive them back into the desolation of their own making."

The Chair-mammal looked down and spoke softly. "Perhaps we lack the wisdom of our ancient forefathers. We have been unable to ascertain a non-violent third solution. It is with great solemnity and sadness that I present the unanimous decision of the council." He again looked around. "We fight."

The forest animals erupted in a cheer. Those that had fists, raised them in the air. Some howled at the moon. Others stomped their feet. A chorus of voices raised together in a chant, "We Fight! We Fight!"

. . .

Meanwhile, deep inside the southern forest, thousands of beetles gathered around the stump of a recently fallen tree. A flat rock lay in the

middle of the stump. Standing on top of the rock
was a solitary Pine Beetle. They called him
Bruno, and he was a cruel brute of a beetle. His
shiny black carapace was marked by many
scars. He was surrounded by Tiger Beetles who
served as his guards and enforcers. Hundreds
more Tiger Beetles were scattered through the
crowd.

The crowd was restless. They were hungry.
Some were in the early stages of starvation.
Many were making loud buzzing noises. Bruno

raised his two front legs, and the crowd became silent. "My fellow beetles," he began, in a raspy voice. "In our homeland, you suffered." A murmur of assent arose from the crowd.

"In our homeland, the mammals and birds attacked us relentlessly." The crowd shouted in agreement.

"Our homeland was destroyed, and they blamed us. They blamed every beetle." The crowd roared.

"Now all we want is refuge and asylum in this forest of great resources and prosperity. We brought them gifts of cheap fertilizer, but now they reject us. All we asked for was our fair share, and they treat us like scum. They want to send us back into starvation." The buzzing beetles added to the roar of the crowd.

Bruno stood up on his back legs. He was shouting now, "Death to the mammals!" The crowd erupted in chanting, "Death to the mammals. Death to the mammals." Then, they began chanting his name, "Bruno, Bruno, Bruno."

# Glossary

Harmony: agreement or concord.

Prosper: successful or fortunate, thrive, flourish.

Appease: pacify or placate (someone) by acceding to their demands. to make concessions to.

Imminent: about to happen.

Desolation: a state of complete emptiness or destruction.

Ascertain: find (something) out for certain; make sure of something.

Solemnity: the state or quality of being serious and dignified.

Unanimous: (of two or more people) fully in agreement with each other.

Pine Beetles: a species of bark beetle native to the forests of western North America from Mexico to central British Columbia. It has a hard, black exoskeleton.

Carapace: the hard upper shell.

Tiger Beetles: a large group of beetles known for their aggressive predatory habits and running speed.

Raspy: hoarse or harsh-sounding.

Assent: the expression of approval or agreement.

Refuge: shelter or protection from danger or distress.

Asylum: the protection granted by a nation to someone who has left their native country as a political refugee.

# 13. The Third Way

Ralph crawled away from the council meeting in deep sadness. Even Mama was caught up in the call to war. He wished his Grandpapa was still alive so that he could seek his advice. Maybe Grandpapa would know of a different solution, one that would not result in bloodshed and the potential deaths of many of his friends. Now, there was no one to whom he could turn.

Ralph wandered aimlessly deep into the forest, lost in thought. He was about to turn back when he saw movement on the ground. A tiny Pine Beetle was walking around in circles, stirring up the pine needles. Ralph quickly looked around. *Has the invasion started already?* He could see no other beetles, so he started to relax.

Ralph flattened himself on the ground in front of the beetle. It rose up on its back legs as if to defend itself. Ralph spoke softly, "Hello, little beetle. Are you lost?"

The tiny Pine Beetle began to cry. "I was snatched from my family by a big flying creature. It held me in its beak and tried to crush me. I could feel my shell cracking and thought I was going to die. The creature flew and flew and chewed and chewed. After a long while, the creature gave up and dropped me. I have been wandering around ever since. Do you know where my family is?"

"No, little one. I am not sure, but I might have an idea. Do you remember anything about where your family was when you were abducted?" The beetle thought for a few moments. He said, "All I remember, is that there was a beautiful forest with delicious trees. Then the trees started getting sick."

"I think I know where to find your family. Would you like me to take you there?" The beetle looked at him suspiciously. "You are a mammal. Don't you want to eat me?" Ralph chuckled and said, "No, little one. I like to eat pine nuts. I have never eaten a beetle." The beetle lowered itself onto the rest of his legs. "Bruno said you would eat us. I wanna go home. Please, sir, take me home."

Ralph nodded. "Okay then. Crawl onto my back, and I will fly you home." The little beetle looked at him sideways. "I may be young, but I know mammals cannot fly." Ralph laughed. "Technically, you are correct. I am a flying squirrel, but I cannot fly. I can only glide long distances. It is like flying, but without all the flapping." The little beetle replied, "Well, that is good because I did not like all that flapping anyway."

Ralph climbed to the top of a tall tree and launched into the air. The beetle hung on, keeping its eyes buried in Ralph's soft fur. The sun was beginning to rise, spreading its rays across the treetops. Ralph launched from tree to tree. He kept a wary eye on the sky above. He didn't want to run into any owls or have any owls run into him and his passenger.

"Say, little one," Ralph asked, "Do you remember where you were born?" The beetle thought a moment and said, "Yes. We were once in a different forest, far, far away. But the trees all died, and there was no food left. We walked a long way to find the forest where my family is now."

Ralph asked, "Doesn't your family know how to store food for the future?" The little beetle replied, "Why would we store food? There is always another tree to eat." Ralph looked over his shoulder but could not see his passenger. "From what you have been telling me, there is not always another tree to eat. It seems like your people eat and eat until the trees are dead. Do you know how to plant and grow another tree so that you have food for your children?" It seemed like a simple question to Ralph, but the beetle started crying again. "I do not know what you are talking about. All I know is that we eat and move, eat, and move."

Ralph had an idea. Maybe there was a third way to solve the conflict. He turned around and started to glide back home.

# Glossary

<u>Potential:</u> possibility

<u>Abducted</u>: take (someone) away illegally by force or deception; kidnap.

<u>Technically:</u> according to the facts or exact meaning of something; strictly.

# 14. Choice and Change

Ralph scrambled up the next tree and was able to see many miles ahead. The ground below was heating up, and Ralph could smell the thermals. "Hey, little one," he called back to the tiny beetle buried in his fur. "We are going to fly without flapping. I think you will like this. Hang on!" Without waiting for a reply, he launched into the sky. He smelled the changing air and soon was banking into a strong thermal. He continued to turn until he was almost a mile above the treetops.

From this vantage point, he could see the two armies heading toward each other. The mammals were large and powerful, but the beetles had the advantage of numbers. There were thousands of beetles for every mammal! This was going to be a disaster for both sides.

The armies were heading to a large clearing in the forest. The ground was covered in large black boulders, dark gravel, and dirt. Ralph could feel the heat radiating upward as the sunlight heated the clearing. The mammals arrived first and began to set up a defensive perimeter on the northern side. Ralph noticed a circle of beetles moving rapidly toward the clearing. Ralph swooped down and started circling the clearing. If he banked just right, he could almost hover hundreds of feet above.

Ralph shouted to the armies, "Please stop! You don't have to do this." The mammals looked up and saw Ralph, wearing his red superhero shirt, circling overhead. They cheered, thinking Ralph was there to help them win the war. The beetles stopped their advance at the edge of the clearing, but Ralph could see thousands more getting closer.

Ralph shouted, "Beetles, my friends. We can
help you reforest your homeland. We know how
to do it!" He circled again. Thousands of beetles
were looking back and forth at each other and
then at the flying squirrel in the red shirt.
Ralph continued, "We can feed all of you, but
you must say away from our trees. You carry a

fungus that kills them. That is what killed the trees in your homeland."

Ralph circled a third time. He could see that his words were affecting the beetles. "You may stay in our forests, and we will share our supplies with you until your home is restored. You will never have to leave your homeland again." He could see the confusion in their eyes, but they stopped advancing into the clearing. To their amazement, he banked and circled again.

"All you have to do is learn to **take one and plant two**. For every single tree you take, you must plant two more. We can show you how. As you gather your food, you must **eat two and save one**." Ralph was able to hover in place. The beetles wondered why he had not fallen from the sky. Maybe he was a Superhero! Ralph shouted, "With these two principles, you can live in peace with us."

The beetles started murmuring and chanting, "Take one and plant two. Eat two and save one."

Bruno climbed onto a black rock. He began shouting, "No! No! Death to the mammals! Death to the mammals!" But now, none of the beetles repeated his chant. They were mesmerized by the Superhero Flying Squirrel above them.

Ralph spotted movement out of the corner of his eye. At first, he thought it might be an owl coming to kill him. He soon saw that its feathers were almost black. It was a raven. The raven flew past Ralph, swooped down, and snatched Bruno off the rock, and flew off into the distance.

Ralph glided toward the clearing and landed in front of the beetles. "Hi, everyone!" he shouted. "I am Ralph! There is a little fellow on my back who is lost and is looking for his family. Can anyone help?'

The little beetle crawled up on top of Ralph's head and peered into the throng of beetles. Off to the side, a couple of beetles started jumping up and down, waving their front legs. "Jimmy! Jimmy!"

Ralph carried Jimmy to his waiting parents. Ralph said, "You never did tell me your name, little one."

"I'm Jimmy," said the tiny beetle. Ralph said, "Yes. Of course you are. Welcome home, Jimmy."

# Glossary

Advantage: a condition or circumstance that puts one in a favorable or superior position.

Perimeter: the continuous line forming the boundary of a closed geometric figure.

Hover: remain in one place in the air.

Reforest: replant with trees; cover again with forest.

Restored: bring back; reinstate; reinstall.

Principles: a fundamental truth that serves as the foundation for a system of belief

Mesmerized: Spellbound, enchanted, captivated, hypnotized.

# 15. Epilogue

The beetles' homeland was far away, for beetles. It was not so far for mammals. Ralph organized an airlift for dropping seeds onto the beetle's homeland. He recommended that they plant many piñon trees so that there would be a steady supply of pine nuts. The mammals taught the beetles how to plant and care for the trees. The beetles kept their promise and supplied loads of fertilizer the mammals could use in their forest. The beetles saw the wisdom in the two mantras of "*take one, plant two*" and "*eat two, save one.*"

Ralph started a flying school where he taught other flying squirrels how to recognize and soar in thermals. In the right conditions, they could now safely spot owls long before they could attack any small mammals.

Truth be told, however, they learned to soar just for the joy of it.

Of course, they all lived happily ever after.
(Until the next adventure)


-End of Book One-
The Adventures of Ralph,
the Superhero Flying Squirrel

I hope you enjoyed reading this book. If you did, please leave a short review on the Amazon website so that others may learn about this book. Ralph will be eternally grateful.

If you like my writing, you may access my novels here:

https://scottsindelarbooks.com/

# Acknowledgements

I wish to thank my loving wife, the fascinating, fetching, and ever exuberant Susan. She read and re-read my drafts, making cogent suggestions, providing needed criticisms, and making corrections of my punctuation. You are my Superheroine.

I also thank my father-in-law, who, while taking my daughter on a walk, spotted a squirrel and named it Ralph for her. Thank you, Dick. Your memories live on.

Finally, thank you to my fellow pilots of hang gliders and trikes. You opened my eyes to the joy and freedom of soaring up to the clouds.

And to Brad, who taught me how to land.

Made in the USA
Middletown, DE
31 March 2021

36752499R00049